Little Diva

To my inspiration, the "Little Divas" in my life,
Celia Rose and Zaya LaChanze.
And to my Langston.

—LACHANZE

To Dobbin and Chloe.

—BRIAN PINKNEY

A FEIWEL AND FRIENDS BOOK
An Imprint of Macmillan

Library of Congress Cataloging-in-Publication Data Available

ISBN: 978-0-312-37010-7

Book design by April Ward

Feiwel and Friends logo designed by Filomena Tuosto

First Edition: 2010

1 3 5 7 9 10 8 6 4 2

www.feiwelandfriends.com

Little Diva

LaChanze

illustrated by Brian Pinkney

FEIWEL AND FRIENDS
NEW YORK

My name is **Nena** and I'm a D.I.T.—
that's a Diva-in-Training.

Divas can act and sing and dance. And when I grow up,
I want to be a diva just like my mommy.

She's a **real** diva—a **Broadway star!**

Mommy says divas
have to work very,
very hard from
morning 'til night.
But that sounds
like **fun** to me.

Divas need lots of rest,
so even when I'm sleeping,
I'm in training.

Maybe **that's** why it's SO HARD to wake up
in the morning. Right, Hunchy?

D.I.T.s start the day with a healthy breakfast. Mommy makes the **best** in the world: chicken apple sausage, scrambled eggs with cheese, and strawberries on the side.

My **favorite!**

She even makes lemon tea with honey because it's good for my voice. My nana says, "You don't need any help in **that** department!"

Nana likes quiet D.I.T.s.

After breakfast, I get dressed. A real diva always wears outfits that are **special** and **stylish** and not like anyone else's. That's why I'm trying on Mommy's clothes.

I turn one way, and then the other.

Mommy takes one look at me and says,
"Work it, my little D.I.T."

My nana says
I'm making her **dizzy**.

I finish just
as Mommy starts
practicing her yoga.
She likes when we
do it together.

She thinks yoga is very relaxing,
but I still have a lot to learn,
because it's **NOT**
very relaxing for me.

Today, my mommy has a matinee—an afternoon show—and I get to go to the theatre with her. I **LOVE** it here.

Actors make magic onstage . . .

and the crew makes
magic backstage.

Everyone has a special job to do.
D.I.T.s have to know all about what
goes on, so I pay close attention.

My favorite part backstage is the
wardrobe department. There are
so many costumes . . .

and makeup and wigs.
I really feel like a **TRUE** diva here.

All the musicians are crowded down in the orchestra pit,
which is in front of the stage and almost under it.

Steve, the coolest guitar
player, lets ME try tuning up.
He says it helps my ear.

So, why is everyone else
covering **their** ears?

Finally, the stage manager starts the countdown. . . .

I call out, **"PLACES!!!"** and then . . .

it's **showtime!**

I rush to my special D.I.T.
seat on the side of the stage
so I can see everything.

Here comes my mommy.
WOW! She looks **SO** different.

It's magic
FOR SURE!

At the end of the show, the actors take their bows. I've been practicing mine.

Mommy says a real diva **NEVER** bows too long, but I could bow forever. I imagine the day when the audience will clap and cheer. "Nena, we love you, Diva! **You are AMAZING!**"

But I have a long way to go before that day.

Back home, I sing all the songs and repeat my favorite lines for Nana and Hunchy.

Hunchy starts singing, but Nana says, "Hush, Hunchy. Let **Nena** sing."

After dinner, Mommy has to go back to the theatre for her second show. I really miss my mommy when she leaves at night. That's when I want her all to myself.

Before Mommy goes, she kisses my cheek,
my nose, my head, and my chin. "Have sugar,
apple, honey, strawberry ice cream sundae
dreams tonight," she sings.

Then we do the
NO BAD DREAMS
dance together.

Hunchy and I curl up to sleep,
and Nana gives me my milk.

What a day!
Divas sure do work hard!

Tomorrow, maybe
I'll make up my own show so
Mommy can watch ME.

"Work it, my little D.I.T.," she'll say.
And I will.

This Little Diva is on her way.